Nelson at Sea

Nelson at Sea

SIMON WESTON
in collaboration with David FitzGerald

Illustrated by
Jac Jones

Pont

Published in 2011 by Pont Books, an imprint of
Gomer Press, Llandysul, Ceredigion, SA44 4JL

ISBN 978-1-84851-315-0
A CIP record for this title is available from the British Library.

This book is published with the financial support of the
Welsh Books Council.

Printed and bound in Wales at
Gomer Press, Llandysul, Ceredigion

Chapter One

Hello there, and welcome back to my stable at the St Mary Dairy in Pont-y-cary, the home I share with two rats called Rhodri and Rhys...and a pigeon with no sense of direction. Next door lives Cardigan, the ex-racehorse. He sleeps a lot! In fact he doesn't do much else.

Nearby, in the pond, live some newts and a frog in a bow tie who thinks he's a special agent...Oh, and a bunch of rugby-playing ducks called the All Quacks! So...just a normal stable-yard really!

I thought that when I retired from pulling the last horse-drawn milk float in Wales, life would get easier, but let me tell you about what happened last Thursday.

Mike the Milk, my owner, came home from his round in 'Floatie', his new electric milk float. He was carrying a large pile of books with him, and whistling. 'Hello, Nelson,' he said in a cheery voice. 'It's time to book a holiday. But keep it to yourself.' And he vanished into the kitchen.

Holiday...HOLIDAY? He has never been on holiday before!

I banged a hoof on Cardigan's stable door. The snoring stopped and Cardigan's straw-covered head slowly appeared. 'What is it?' he said, yawning. 'Is there a fire?'

'No,' I said. 'Don't tell anyone but Mike has just come home in a really good mood: he says he is booking his holidays.'

'Cooking a Bolognese...yummy,' said Cardigan. 'I love spaghetti. Don't worry. I won't tell a soul. Mike's secret is safe with me. Not a word will pasta my lips.' He started to giggle. 'Pasta my lips...spaghetti...get it?'

I forgot to tell you that Cardigan is very old and very deaf and, at times, very silly.

'No, no, no!' I shouted. 'Holidays...Mike is going on his HOLIDAYS.'

Well, so much for keeping it quiet; the whole stable-yard heard me. The

'Holiday?'

NELSON

rats, Rhodri and Rhys, came running from the reeds around the duck pond. Behind them waddled the All Quacks with their trainer, Sir Francis Drake. Flight Lieutenant Pigeon fluttered down from the rafters of my barn and James Pond, the lunatic frog, hopped out of my drinking bucket. I wish he wouldn't wash his flippers in there!

'Holiday?' squeaked Rhodri and Rhys.

'Holiday?' gulped James Pond, fiddling with his bow tie.

'Holiday?' quacked the ducks.

I held my hoof up for quiet but everyone started jumping up and down, shouting: 'Holiday...holiday...holiday!'

After about five minutes, Rhodri asked a very good question. 'Where's he taking us?'

I shrugged. 'He didn't say. He just had a huge pile of holiday books and he's gone into the kitchen to read them. He said there's nothing like a good brochure.'

'You sure?' said Rhys.

'No...*brochure*,' said Rhodri.

'That's a French word,' said Flight Lieutenant Pigeon.

'He's taking us all to France?' squeaked Rhys.

'I hope not,' said James Pond, crossing his legs.

'Why not?' I said. 'France is lovely.'

But the pigeon fluttered over onto my neck and whispered in my ear. 'They eat frogs' legs in France,' he hissed.

'Oh...right!' I said. 'That's a very good point.'

'And horse meat,' added Sir Francis Drake.

That was an even better point. I quickly changed direction. 'I expect he might be thinking of a holiday closer to home, like . . . er . . . like Devon, for example.'

'Sir Francis Drake came from Devon,' said Sir Francis, puffing out his feathers. 'He was a very important sailor and my mother named me after him.'

'They make the best cream teas in Devon,' said Flight Lieutenant Pigeon. 'I flew there once on my way from London to Newport.'

Sir Francis looked puzzled and was about to say something but I stopped him. As I said, Flight Lieutenant Pigeon has no sense of direction.

'Stopped for a spot of lunch,' he went on. 'Stayed for a cream tea. Huge fresh scones, inches of Devon clotted cream and then a big blob of strawberry jam on top.' His eyes took on a faraway look as he recalled other memorable meals from different parts of the country. 'Scotch pancakes from Cardiff . . . bara brith from Edinburgh . . . Yorkshire pudding from Oxford!'

Rhodri started to dribble and lick his whiskers. 'I want to go to Devon for the cream teas.'

'So do I,' said his brother. 'But are they very high? My legs are only little and I'm not very good at climbing!'

'Climbing what?' I said.

'Trees!' he said.

'What trees?'

Rhys stamped his paw. 'The cream trees,' he said impatiently. 'You know, the cream trees from Devon,' and he rubbed his little tummy.

Have you ever been sorry you started a conversation?

'Listen,' I said to the entire yard. 'We don't know where Mike is going. Let's just wait. I'm sure he will tell us soon.'

'Do you want us to sneak into the house and take a peek?' said Rhys.

'Now, you two,' I said, wagging a hoof in the rats' direction. 'I have told you before to keep your whiskers out of other people's business. You know what happened the last time you meddled in Mike's affairs. I ended up pulling a state carriage for Prince Charles. I got on the television, I got on the radio, I got in the papers...and I got into trouble.'

'We would only have a quick peek,' said Rhodri.

'No,' I said firmly. 'Absolutely not! Definitely no, no way.' I shuffled my hooves. 'Well, maybe just a quick peek then.'

'Right,' said Rhodri. 'Can I borrow the All Quacks and James Pond?'

Everyone nodded and off they all marched. I settled down at my stable door to watch proceedings. First the ducks formed a small pyramid and gave James a bunk-up onto the kitchen windowsill so he could keep a lookout!

'Brilliant,' said Rhodri. 'Shout if you see Mike. Now, can all the ducks stand on each other's shoulders please so that Rhys can climb up to the door handle?'

The ducks did as they were told and slowly, carefully, Rhys used them as a sort of feather-covered ladder. Up and up he climbed, duck after duck, until he reached the top. Then all the ducks began to wobble.

'No wobbling!' cried Rhys.

'You're too heavy,' shouted Rhodri. 'Just grab the door handle.'

'I'm trying,' shouted Rhys and made a leap for the door.

Meanwhile, James Pond had stuck his head round the open kitchen window to see if Mike the Milk was inside. He hopped in and then hopped out again and shouted that the coast was clear.

'Are you going to tell them or shall I?' Cardigan had joined me at the stable door and was watching the

scene: Rhys clinging to the door handle, the ducks struggling to keep their balance and James Pond shouting instructions from the kitchen.

'What?' I said. 'Tell them that the window's open and James is already inside! No, there's nothing worth watching on the telly: let's stay here for a little bit longer.'

In fact, we watched for nearly ten minutes as the ducks tried again and again to prop up the dangling rat, whilst James Pond kept hopping in and out of the window.

I looked at Cardigan and said, 'It's no use. I am going to have to go over there myself and sort this out.'

'Might be an idea,' he said, yawning. 'Come and wake me if you find out where we're going.' And then he added, 'I hope it isn't far. If it takes that lot ten minutes to get through the back door, how long will it take to get to the airport?'

Chapter Two

Mike was having forty winks upstairs and didn't hear all the hullabaloo. Just as I reached the ducks, James Pond must have jumped down from the windowsill to the door handle, and swung the door open. As he did so, all the ducks fell in on top of him. Rhys, who was still holding the handle on the other side, flew through the air and landed on the kitchen counter. Sliding along on his bottom, he sped past the bread bin, tore past the toaster, bounced off the boxes of cornflakes and finally skidded into the sink, where he stopped ... and landed in a basin full of warm soapy water.

I peered into the kitchen to see Rhys climbing out of the sink, covered in foam. He stood up and wiped the suds off the end of his nose. 'Rhodri,' he squeaked. 'It's horrible! I'm all clean.'

Rhodri was standing right beside me. 'Oh dear,' he said. 'My brother doesn't sound very happy. He wasn't due a bath until next April.'

I must explain here that rats do not always deserve their reputation for being dirty animals. Pet rats can be very clean indeed, but Rhys? I don't think so. 'Listen,' I said to Rhodri. 'I can see Mike's pile of holiday brochures on the kitchen table. Take James Pond with you, have a quick look and then get out. Rhys, come back with me and I will find you a towel.'

Rhys squelched his way out of the kitchen while his brother and the frog hopped up onto the table.

It was another five minutes before James and Rhodri appeared at my stable door eager to tell me what they had seen. Rhys was now all dry and fluffy, and had already started rolling around in the mud to stick his fur down.

'I hate soap and water,' he said, shuddering, and to make himself feel better, he dragged his tail through some drain water and flicked a couple of drops behind his ears.

It wasn't long before the rest of the yard came running, quacking and fluttering, and sat down. I gave Cardigan another nudge to wake him up.

'Well?' I said to my two spies.

'Wow,' squeaked Rhodri.

'Yes, wow,' said James.

'Well, where are we going?'

'We don't know,' they said together. 'We can't read!'

'But we did see some pictures,' said James. 'There was a horse.'

'Horse-tralia?' suggested Rhys.

'Don't be silly,' I said.

He tried again. 'Horse-tria?'

I folded my hooves and gave him one of my best stares. 'We have had this conversation before. Horses do not come from Horse-tralia or Horse-tria. Hamsters do not come from Hamsterdam! Jam does not come from Jamaica and seals do not come from New Sealand...right?'

'Don't turkeys come from Turkey then?' said Rhodri.

'NO!' everyone shouted. 'Now, will you get on with it?'

'What else can you remember?' I said.

'Well...' Rhodri scratched his head for a while. 'There was an o. At the end. O was the very last letter.'

'O?' I said.

'O!' he repeated.

'Seven?' asked James Pond hopefully. 'Double O Seven?'

'No, just o,' said Rhodri.

There was a slight pause and then we all said, 'Oh!'

'Can you remember anything else?'

'There was a picture of the sea,' said James.

'And a tree,' added Rhodri. 'And a beach with a sort of fairground with rides and things.'

Cardigan coughed. 'I think I might know where that is.'

We all looked at him and waited.

'Orlando,' he announced.

'Wow!' gasped the rats.

'Wow!' said the ducks.

'Wow!' echoed Flight Lieutenant Pigeon. 'Germany.'

'Florida,' corrected Cardigan.

'Oh, Thailand,' said the pigeon.

'AMERICA,' said Cardigan slowly. 'Florida is hot and sunny and has beautiful beaches. It's got Disneyland. That's a sort of giant fairground.'

'What else? What else?' we all wanted to know.

'Well, it's a long way from Wales,' he said. 'We will have to fly.'

'Fly!' said the ducks.

'But when we get there we can all go for a swim,' he continued.

'Swim!' exclaimed the ducks.

'In water?' shuddered Rhys.

'And then we can go to Disneyland and meet Donald: he's a duck.'

'Fly, swim and meet a duck,' said Sir Francis, looking really bored. 'Oh great. I can't wait.'

'Well, there's Mickey as well. He's a mouse.'

'Wonderful,' sighed Rhodri, yawning.

'You're not selling it to us,' said Rhys. 'Florida sounds really dull.'

Suddenly we heard a loud voice. 'What is going on here?'

Well, I nearly jumped out of my harness. There was Mike at the kitchen door, standing with his arms folded, listening to us. 'Why is my back door open? Why are there duck feathers on my floor? And why is there a trail of washing-up foam all over my kitchen work-top?'

I raised my hoof and said it was my fault. I told him that we were very sorry but we just wanted to know where we were going on holiday.

'Is it Florida?' asked Rhys, sounding really depressed.

'We're not interested in meeting celebrity mice!' said Rhodri.

'Or famous ducks,' added Sir Francis.

Mike scratched his head. 'Mice, ducks, Florida...what are you lot talking about?'

'Orlando,' I said. 'Rhodri saw an o and we guessed it must be Orlando.'

Mike started to chuckle. 'It's not Orlando,' he smiled. 'It's Llandudno! I've just booked it.'

We all turned and glared at Rhodri. 'What?' he protested, putting his little paws in the air. 'All I said was that I saw an *o*.'

'We're off to Llandudno for a long weekend in a bed-and-breakfast place on the sea front,' Mike explained. 'I've just finished arranging it.'

'Llandudno! Wow! I can't wait!' I said. 'Mammy told me all about Llandudno. It's in north Wales near Horse-on-Sea. She stayed there once.'

'I think you mean Rhos-on-Sea,' said Mike quietly.

'Like I said, Horse-on-Sea,' I replied. 'When are we going?'

'Not "we", Nelson. "Me"...' mumbled Mike, '...and about twenty-five others. It's the fifth anniversary of UM.'

Sir Francis ruffled his feathers. 'UM?'

'*Union of Milkmen*,' muttered Mike. 'We used to be called the *British Union of Milkmen* but we dropped the *British*.'

I could not believe my ears. I looked over at Rhys and Rhodri. Their whiskers were quivering with disappointment. Even Flight Lieutenant

Pigeon seemed to have lost his usual dizziness. And as for James, I don't think I've ever seen him look so sad. I looked back at Mike. 'What's going to happen to us when you're away? You'd never leave us on our own.'

'I'm going on Friday morning and my cousin Mervyn will come over on Friday evening. He'll do the milk round on Saturday. You'll be fine. It's only for the weekend.'

Could it get any worse? Merv the Milk isn't like Mike at all. He's mean and mad and moody. He won't even talk to us.

'What about the newts?' I asked. 'The last time Merv looked after the dairy, they staged a sit-in and wouldn't come out of the pond.'

'That won't be a problem this time,' said Mike. 'They'll be on holiday too.'

'They're going on holiday?' I snorted. 'They never told us.'

'That's because they don't speak,' said Mike. 'They are mute newts, remember? They're going to a holiday camp. I helped them with the booking forms.'

'Holiday camp! Where?' I asked.

'Pond-tins of course,' said Mike. 'Where else would you expect newts to stay? Pontins?'

Suddenly the phone rang from the living room and Mike hurried in to answer it, leaving a very fed-up set of stablemates behind him.

Chapter Three

Everyone looked at me as if I would know what to do.

'We wanted to go on holiday,' said Rhys in a very sad and quiet voice.

'We all did,' said Sir Francis.

The All Quacks nodded in agreement.

'Mission cancelled,' muttered James Pond.

'I am completely lost,' said Flight Lieutenant Pigeon. 'For words, I mean.'

'We could always book our own holiday,' said Cardigan thoughtfully.

I looked at him. 'Mike would go mad!' I said.

'He'll never find out, if we go at the same time as he does. I've got my saddle-top computer: we can look for holidays online and pay over the phone with my HSBC card.'

'What's an HSBC card?' asked Rhodri.

'Horse and Stable Banking Company.'

'You have a bank account?' I said.

Cardigan nodded. 'I've had one for years. That's where all my racing prize-money is. These days I bank online.'

I was stunned. I knew that Cardigan had a mobile phone, but I didn't know that he used the internet.

We all looked at each other. There was a slight pause and then everyone made a mad dash for Cardigan's stable. Ducks, rats, a frog, a pigeon and two horses all crammed in as Cardigan used his computer to find the Pont-y-cary travel agent, Terrific Trefor Thomas Total Travel Tours.

'Right, we've only got a weekend,' said Cardigan. 'So it will have to be somewhere close...like...'

'Llandudno?' suggested Rhodri.

We all looked at him and he went red. 'Oh yes, Mike is going to be there.'

'Tenby,' declared Cardigan.

'Tenby?' we all said as we crowded around the screen.

'Lovely place,' said Cardigan. 'My father was in a racing stable there. Here, have a look at the pictures of the sea front.'

I must admit that it did look very nice.

'Shall I see if there's a trip this weekend?' asked Cardigan, picking up his mobile phone. 'But first, could you all go outside for a moment? It's getting a bit hot in here.'

We all trooped out and strained our ears to hear what he was saying.

'He's reading out numbers from his card,' said Rhodri.

'Is that because we're going to Ten-by?' asked Rhys.

Fortunately, Cardigan ended his call at that moment and we all went back in. He was smiling. 'We are booked. On Friday afternoon a minibus from Terrific Trefor Thomas Total Travel Tours will come and pick us up.'

Everybody cheered and clapped and bounced up and down.

'What shall we take with us?' said Rhodri and Rhys excitedly.

I thought for a moment. 'A sunhat. I don't want you getting burnt.'

'But rats don't wear hats,' complained Rhys. 'Not even in the sun.'

'Well, you should. Sunhats are important, and so is suncream,' I explained. I found a pencil and paper and started to make a list. 'Suncream – *Rats Factor* – and two little rat hats.'

'What else?' said Rhodri.

'Better bring your buckets and spades . . . a beach ball . . . some swimming trunks and a towel, a rubber ring, and . . .'

Both Rhodri and Rhys had started to look really sad. They sat there twiddling their paws.

'What's wrong?'

Rhodri was the first to speak. 'When you say swimming trunks, you mean trunks to swim in, don't you?'

It was then that it hit me. 'You two can't swim, can you?'

They shook their heads. 'We don't even like taking baths,' said Rhys.

'Right,' I said. Something had to be done. I turned to Sir Francis Drake. 'Could you do me a big favour?' I said and I whispered in his ear.

'What?' said Sir Francis, looking at the rats and shaking his head. 'Wait there!' He waddled over to the kitchen and knocked on the door.

'Do you have any rubber gloves for washing up?' he asked when Mike came to the door. 'Oh, and some cork too, and could you help me cut things out with the scissors please?'

Mike looked a bit puzzled at first but when Sir Francis explained what it was for, he was really enthusiastic. 'Swimming lessons are always a good idea,' he said. 'Glad to help. Rhodri and Rhys, you'd better come into the kitchen.' And in they went.

Sir Francis waddled back to me and gave me the thumbs-up with his wing feathers. 'While Mike's away on holiday we can teach the rats to swim,' he winked. 'It will help pass the weekend.'

But I had to ask why he needed rubber gloves, scissors and cork.

'Don't worry,' was all he would say. 'All will be revealed.'

Well, ten long minutes passed! Then twenty, and then thirty, but suddenly the kitchen door opened and out came Mike with a big smile on his face. 'Come on, you two,' he said, and slowly two miniature bathers in identical costumes walked out into the yard. What a sight! Rhodri and Rhys were wearing bright-yellow swimming trunks which Mike had made by cutting up the rubber gloves. He had created swimming hats for them too and finally, with some cork from an old floor tile, he had made floats for a pair of armbands. Rhodri and Rhys looked truly 'rat-diculous'.

'Over to the pond and wait by the water's edge,' ordered Sir Francis. The rats dragged their paws to a clearing in the reeds.

'Looks cold,' said Rhys.

'Looks wet,' said Rhodri.

Sir Francis waddled over and cleared his throat. 'Lesson one. Now, I want you to walk into the water slowly, making sure it is not too deep for you.'

Rhodri and Rhys held paws and both dipped their toes in.

'Brrrrrrrrrrrrrrrrrrrr!' shivered Rhys. 'Cooooooooolllllld!'

'Weeeeeeeeettttttttttt,' shuddered Rhodri. 'I can't do this.'

'It will be all right once you are in,' said Sir Francis.

Rhodri smiled. 'I bet my brother wants to go first.'

'What?' said Rhys just as Rhodri gave him a push.

Rhodri laughed and laughed and laughed as Rhys splashed and coughed and spluttered.

The water was only a few inches deep but Sir Francis was really angry. 'Never push anyone into water,' he quacked loudly.

'And never pull anyone in, either,' said Rhys, tugging at his brother's tail. A small wave of water rose into the air as Rhodri did a nosedive into the pond.

'Now stop it, you two,' quacked Sir Francis crossly. 'We are not going to get anywhere with this sort of behaviour.'

Things calmed down after that and for the next hour or so the rats bobbed up and down in the pond. They complained and sulked at first but after a while they actually seemed to be enjoying it. Sir Francis was quacking out orders and, for once in their lives, the rats were listening and doing what they were told. Rhodri was pretty good at the doggy paddle – or ratty paddle – and Rhys could do the crawl.

At the end of the lesson, Sir Francis, James Pond and all the other water creatures gave the rats a round of applause when they took off their cork floats and swam a few uncertain strokes to the shore.

'Early days. We will practise on holiday,' whispered Sir Francis so that Mike wouldn't hear, and then he said more loudly: 'Well done, you rats!'

That evening, two very sleepy and surprisingly clean rats climbed into my straw in the stable. The brothers were boasting to each other about which of them was going to swim the entire length of the pond before leaving the following day. I pointed out that it was a bit early for that though I was so proud that they were learning to swim. 'But,' I added, 'don't even think about going near the water without a grown-up to watch you.'

'Will there be boats at Tenby?' asked Rhys. 'Can we go sailing?'

I thought for a moment. 'There might be,' I said. 'But you will have to practise your swimming first. Now try and get some sleep.'

They snuggled down. 'We could become famous sailors,' said Rhodri, yawning. 'We could go around the world in a ratamaran.'

'What's a ratamaran?' asked Rhys.

'It's like two boats joined together. I saw it on TV. They called it a twin-hulled ratamaran.'

'Not a ratamaran, silly. That's a *cat*amaran,' explained Rhys. 'So we won't be going near one of those, will we?'

'What are you two on about?' I said, tucking them in.

'Sailing,' said Rhodri. 'We could become pirates like Captain Jack Sparrow. Is he related to Flight Lieutenant Pigeon?'

'I don't think so,' I said. 'Now go to sleep. We all have a long day tomorrow and we haven't packed yet.'

Chapter Four

At ten o'clock the next morning, Mike was waiting for the coach with all his mates from UM. Right on time, it pulled up outside the dairy gates and we all crowded round to wave goodbye.

'Now, Merv will be here later on today. Do you think you can all behave until he arrives?' asked Mike.

'Yes,' we said.

'And don't give him any trouble when he is trying to work.'

'No,' we chorused.

'He won't know we're here,' said Rhys, and Rhodri sniggered.

'Have a great time in Tenby,' I shouted.

Everyone started to cough and shout goodbye. 'Llandudno, I mean,' I called after him but Mike was already on the bus. I don't think he heard me.

With a roar of the engine he was gone. We all looked at each other. 'Time to pack,' I said and everybody scampered, hopped or waddled off.

Well, let me give you a little bit of advice. Never ask a rat to pack his own bag. Who would take with them on holiday a marble, a rubber band, six leaves and a pen with no ink! Mind you, James Pond the potty frog wanted to bring some slime, and his secret two-way radio, which we all know is the remote control to Mike's telly. He's been looking for that for months!

I found my swimming shorts, size XXXXXXXXXXXXXXL, which I must admit are a bit tight, and threw them into a case. Next I dusted off a pair of sunglasses, found a towel, and something to read on the beach . . . I am halfway through *The Horse Whisperer* at the moment. It's the audio version and it's a bit hard to hear.

By mid afternoon we were ready and waiting. Suddenly there was a toot and a minibus drew up outside the gates. A very nice young man with a smart green uniform stepped out and opened the door and introduced himself. 'Hello,' he said. 'I'm Ivor the Driver from Terrific Trefor Thomas Total Travel Tours. All aboard for Tenby.'

I don't think Ivor the Driver from Terrific Trefor Thomas Total Travel Tours has ever seen a stampede before or witnessed how a shire horse gets into a minibus. It took about twenty minutes to settle everybody, with me in the front seat so I could read the map and keep James Pond in a bucket between my hooves. Rhodri and Rhys, Cardigan, Sir Francis Drake and all the other ducks spread themselves around the seats while Flight Lieutenant Pigeon said he would fly along behind just in case 'we' got lost! But when we turned left out of the dairy and he turned right, we sat him down at the back of the bus and told him not to move until we got to Tenby.

There was a lot of traffic and the journey took a long time, so Rhodri and Rhys played 'I Spy'. Rhys said he'd spotted something beginning with A. It took forty-five minutes until his brother finally gave in. The answer was 'a tractor'. Then Rhodri found something that also began with A and, thirty minutes later, his brother correctly guessed it: 'another tractor'. As I said, it was a long, long trip.

But we made it and found our guest house which was called *Trem y Môr*. 'It means "Sea View",' I whispered to Sir Francis Drake.

'Well, why doesn't it say so then?' he quacked.

'It does,' I said. 'In Welsh. And in English on the other side,' I added.

Ivor the Driver parked up and started to unload cases, ducks and Cardigan. Then the owner of the guest house came out to welcome us.

'Hello,' she said. 'My name is Rhonda Pugh, but people call me Pugh the View. Welcome to my little guest house. We cater for a range of different guests, just like yourselves. We are in the *Hay-Hay* handbook. We've got a three-horseshoe rating.'

Ivor the Driver placed the last of the cases, and a duck, in the doorway. He waved goodbye and promised to be back on Sunday afternoon.

Ms Pugh opened a large book and started to read. 'I have one single room, an en-suite stable, two holes in the skirting board, a deluxe pond with shower, and a sea-facing perch. Is everybody happy?'

We all said yes.

'Dinner is at 6.30 p.m. in our dining room. Our chef specialises in *haute cuisine*.'

I liked the sound of that and said so. 'Oat cuisine. Home from home.'

'Dinner, in a dining room?' said Rhys. 'If it's home from home, can't we just go through the bins?'

'No,' I said. 'And, James, wait to be served; don't go catching it yourself as it flies by. I want the best manners from all of you.'

'I'll just get someone to come and take your cases,' said Ms Pugh the View.

It didn't take long for us all to settle in. Flight Lieutenant Pigeon said his perch was very comfortable and the ducks and James Pond all took turns to use the shower and deluxe pond.

The rats snuggled into their holes in the skirting board and I must say the stable was just as good as the one I had at home in Pont-y-cary but not quite as posh as the Royal Mews in London. There was lots of fresh straw, a hoof polisher, flat-screen television and a thing called a jacuzzi! Cardigan and I tried to drink the water but it was too bubbly and it made us burp!

Dinner was great. We all made sure we were on our best behaviour as we had to choose from something called a menu. Cardigan and I had oats à la bag. The two rats had ratatouille. The ducks had stale bread drizzled with pond water and Flight Lieutenant Pigeon had a seed soufflé. James had Fly Surprise. The surprise was that the flies flew away. But James remembered

his manners and introduced himself politely to all the other diners as he hopped over their tables, trying to catch his dinner.

That night we slept very well and next day, after breakfast, we all headed for the seafront. 'What shall we do first?' I asked the group.

Rhodri and Rhys had been looking at some colourful leaflets they had found at the guest house and suddenly Rhodri said, 'Can we visit the superloo?'

'Superloo?'

'Yes, the big toilet, silly!' said Rhodri, showing me his leaflet. 'There is one around here that sticks out into the sea.'

'That's the lifeboat station. Where did you get the idea that it was a toilet?' I asked, looking at the picture.

'It says so!' said Rhys, joining in.

I have to say that neither of the rats can read very well and they tend to make it up by spotting the letters they know. They get very excited if they think they've found something rude.

'Look,' they said. 'Look!'

'Hmm,' I replied, looking at them sternly. 'That says Tenby Pier. It's got nothing to do with peeing! A pier is a sort of walkway on stilts. Lots of them were built when Queen Victoria was alive, a long time ago. You can walk right out into the bay and the sea is underneath you.'

The rats immediately wanted to walk along the pier.

'You are a bit late,' I said, handing back the leaflet. 'Tenby Pier closed nearly seventy years ago. The RNLI have a new lifeboat station there now.'

Their little whiskers drooped.

'But there is lots more to do,' I said, 'like . . . like . . . like visiting the seaside sweet shop.'

The rats squeaked and ran off along the seafront, sniffing at windows, looking for sweets. The rest of us wandered along behind them. It was lovely to be at the seaside and Tenby was an excellent choice for a holiday.

'Well done,' I said to my old friend. 'This is going to be a great weekend.'

'I hope so. I do like holidays,' Cardigan said. 'Pity about the pier.'

'Well, we are only seventy years too late,' I said.

'Yes, but I like piers,' persisted Cardigan.

'I like piers too!' said James Pond who was hopping along with us.

'Really?' I said. 'There are some lovely piers in Wales. There is one at the Mumbles, one at Bangor and one in Llandudno where Mike is. And there are lots more. Which of the piers do you like best?'

'Brosnan,' he said. 'Pierce Brosnan,' and hopped off.

I don't know why I bother really.

Chapter Five

The rats had never seen a sweet shop before and, to be honest, the sweet shop had never seen two rats like Rhodri and Rhys.

'Look! Pink clouds!' they cried as they scampered in through the door.

'Pink clouds?' I watched them as they walked up to a big silver food mixer and then saw what they were pointing at. 'Oh, candy floss!'

They each bought a big helping on a stick and walked outside again. Everybody crowded round to watch them. It took about two minutes before the first duck became stuck and then another and another, and then James Pond found his flippers covered in goo.

'Watch what you're doing,' I warned as we all tried to peel a duck free. James Pond managed to hop clear but took a lump of candy floss with him and stood in the middle of the pavement with his little flippers on his hips. He was not a happy frog. He was hot, he was sticky and he was beginning to attract flies. One buzzed around his head.

'Remember your manners,' I said. James nodded and just batted it away.

'Well done,' I congratulated him. 'That reminds me of my favourite James Bond film.'

'What?' he asked with a smile.

'*Live and Let Fly,*' I said, sniggering.

We decided that it might be a good idea for James to go back to the guest house for a shower while the rest of us went to the beach. We would organize a bucket of fresh water for him to sit in later on. Cardigan wanted to have a snooze in the sun as he had been awake for almost two hours and all I wanted was to sit down and do my crossword. So we all headed for a nice sunny spot and I spread out my towel. Cardigan settled down beside me and fell asleep almost at once.

The ducks decided to have a game of beach cricket and persuaded Flight Lieutenant Pigeon and the rats to join them. Everyone played nicely for a while; then it was the pigeon's turn to bat. Yes, you guessed it; he was out for a duck!

The rats soon got bored and said they were going to play in the sea. Putting on their floats and trunks, they were off.

'Don't go too far out!' I shouted at them as they ran across the beach. Soon they had found two bits of driftwood and were surfing in the shallow water right at the sea's edge. I was very proud of those two. They were learning to swim and were really being sensible. It was all too good to be true.

Now, I must admit that I might have nodded off for a moment or two because when I looked up, the tide had gone out, the cricket game had finished and Rhodri and Rhys were nowhere to be seen. I nudged Cardigan, and he woke up with a start. 'What is it?' he yawned.

'Where is everybody?' I asked.

We both started to look about us. 'The potty pigeon is sitting on the railings of that RNLI house-thing,' said Cardigan, waving a hoof up the beach towards what had once been the pier. 'And look: the ducks are bobbing up and down way out there at sea.'

I looked to where he was pointing and I could just see Sir Francis and his team riding the waves, but where were Rhodri and Rhys? I trotted down to the water's edge for a better view and suddenly I spotted them. Two specks clinging onto two bits of wood, drifting away from the shore. They were in deep trouble and they needed help.

I started to wave and shout at Sir Francis until he and the ducks came fluttering over. 'Can you get to the rats?' I said, pointing at the specks which were now even further away. 'They have drifted much too far out.'

Sir Francis just shook his head. 'There are strong currents out there and the rats would be too heavy for us. We will never be able to get them back on our own. You'd better get the RNLI to launch a boat while we fly out and try to keep them afloat by talking to them.'

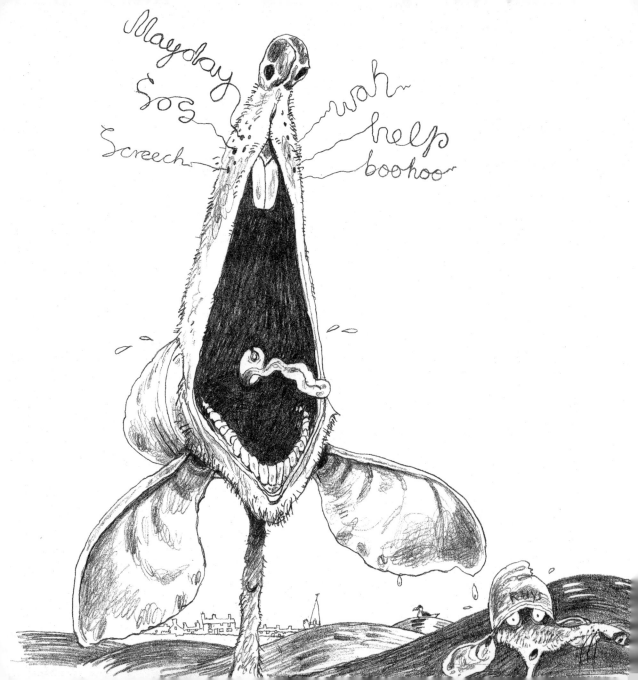

I looked up at the lifeboat station and started to gallop. I could see that Flight Lieutenant Pigeon was talking to an official-looking man. I thought he might know what to do.

Now galloping on a racetrack is one thing. Galloping on hard sand is another. But, believe me, galloping up a sandy beach is something else, especially for a carthorse. My hooves kept sinking into the soft sand and it took every ounce of strength to reach the lifeboat station. I thought my lungs would burst. I had never run that hard in my life. When I got within shouting distance, all I could do was wheeze and point. 'Rats,' I gasped. 'Ducks,' I spluttered. 'Drifting out to sea!'

Flight Lieutenant Pigeon and his new friend just stared down at me. I was so out of puff I don't think they could understand what I was saying. 'Help!' I neighed frantically. 'They're going to drown!'

Suddenly they saw what I was pointing at. The man reached for something that looked a bit like a gun, pointed it to the sky and fired.

Flight Lieutenant Pigeon's beak dropped open. 'Wow,' he said as a bright white light soared into the air. 'That is some firework!'

That's no firework, I thought, panting. That's a flare and I hope he's covered his ears. Too late. There was a huge bang and Flight Lieutenant Pigeon fell off the railings and fluttered down to the beach.

Operation Rat Rescue was on.

Suddenly I could hear the clatter of running boots and then men in bright orange suits and life jackets started to appear from everywhere. Within minutes, three men had put a rubber dinghy into the sea and had started the engine. Then the boat turned away from the shore and began to speed across the waves.

I held my breath as it circled the ducks. They were so far away it was difficult to make out what was going on but soon I saw an orange arm waving and the boat turned back to shore.

Flight Lieutenant Pigeon's friend spoke into a radio. 'Everything OK out there?'

'Roger, Roger . . . two rats rescued,' said a voice and in a short while two very soggy, very sorry, very frightened-looking animals were safely ashore, with Sir Francis and the All Quacks for escort.

Chapter Six

'Well? What have you got to say for yourselves?'

The rats stood there and twiddled their paws. 'We didn't mean to! We just couldn't get back to the beach,' said Rhodri.

'Something was pulling us out!' said Rhys.

'You have got to be careful in the sea,' I scolded. 'There are some very strong currents which can take you way offshore. You could have drowned if it wasn't for these brave people.'

The three men in the dinghy just waved back as they went to put the boat away. Flight Lieutenant Pigeon's friend, who turned out to be the man in charge of the boat, the coxswain, held out two towels for Rhodri and Rhys.

'Thank you, Mr Runlee,' said Rhys, staring at the man's sweater.

'Mr Runlee?' he said, looking down at his badge. 'That says RNLI.'

'His name is Roger Roger,' I corrected.

'My name is Huw,' he said, looking even more confused.

'They called you Roger on the radio.'

'That's "radio speak" for "yes",' he said, laughing. 'We say "Roger" when we understand the message.'

'Why?' everybody wanted to know.

'Well...it's...do you know...I'm not sure!' he said. 'Anyway, I'm Huw, Huw the Crew. I am sorry we had to meet this way but I'm glad it's all ended happily.'

Rhodri and Rhys looked at the water and shuddered.

'You must always tell someone if you are going in the water. You must get a grown-up to check what the local tides are like and where it is safe to swim,' he reminded the rats. 'Why were you going out to sea anyway?'

'To see the island,' said Rhys.

'What island?' asked Huw.

'The big grey one,' said Rhodri, pointing.

We all looked. Way out in the bay was a small mound in the water.

'I don't think that's an island,' said Huw. 'I'd better take a look through the binoculars.' He said nothing for a couple of minutes, then: 'Well! Well! Well!' He put down the binoculars and spoke once more into the radio. 'I think it might be a good idea to launch the big lifeboat.' He turned to us and asked, 'Do you fancy a ride?'

Well, within two shakes of Cardigan's tail, we were being issued with life jackets up in the boathouse and scrambling on board the big orange-and-blue boat at the top of a giant slide. Rhodri and Rhys grabbed the railings. The All Quacks formed a scrum around Flight Lieutenant Pigeon, who didn't look too happy, while Cardigan and I wedged ourselves at the back.

'Does this make us sea horses?' said Cardigan.

There was no time to answer.

'Hang on,' said Huw, starting the engine. The boat began to slip forward, slowly at first, then faster and faster as it hurtled towards the sea until...SPLASH!

'Wowwwww,' said Rhodri.

'Weeeeee,' said Rhys.

'That was fantastic,' I said. 'Better than any ride in Florida.'

As soon as we hit the water, the powerful engine started to push us through the waves and before long we were speeding towards the grey island out in the bay.

'If I'm right,' said Huw the Crew, 'we might need all of you to help out with a little problem.'

'A little problem?' I said, hanging onto Cardigan.

'Well, quite a big problem actually,' smiled Huw. 'His name is Llywelyn and I think he may have got himself stuck again!'

I wasn't sure I knew what he was talking about and, to be honest, I was beginning not to care. I wasn't feeling very well. My stomach was turning over and over as the boat bounced up and down on the waves.

Cardigan noticed that I was going a bit green. 'I thought with a name like Nelson, you would be a better sailor,' he said with a snigger.

'Very funny!' I replied. 'Just keep hanging onto me.'

But within a matter of minutes, Huw was slowing the boat down and guiding us around the great grey island.

Suddenly there was a splash, a swirl of water and the island moved. Slowly, very slowly, a huge eye appeared above the waves. 'Hello!' said a loud booming voice.

'Hello, Llywelyn,' said Huw. 'How are you today?'

There was a short silence as Llywelyn ducked under the waves and then reared up in the water, sending a huge plume of spray into the air.

'You're not an island after all!' said Rhys.

'But what are you?' asked Rhodri.

There was a loud, a very loud, chuckle. 'I'm a whale, a fin whale.'

'A thin whale?' said Rhys. 'You don't look very thin to me! Nelson takes size XXXXXXXL swimming trunks. You must be XXXXXXXXXXXXXXXXX-XXXXXL!'

There was another loud chuckle. 'My name is Llywelyn and I am a "fin whale" not a thin whale. I visit the sea near Tenby from time to time. And, by the way, I don't need to wear swimming trunks!'

'Wow, that's cool,' said Rhys.

'Cool?' said Rhodri. 'He must be absolutely freezing.'

'I'm perfectly comfortable,' replied the fin whale, 'apart from the fact that I'm stuck! I appear to have got myself wedged on a sandbank and, as the tide has gone out, I can't move.'

Everybody started to talk at once. The ducks said they could push; Rhodri and Rhys said they could pull; Flight Lieutenant Pigeon said he could fly for help; Cardigan had his mobile with him and was all for calling the RAC. '*Rescue at sea*, that's what it stands for, isn't it?'

'No, Cardigan. Go back to sleep,' said everybody, talking at the top of their voices. Sir Francis Drake wanted to call the Fire Brigade whilst Huw thought he should radio for a rescue helicopter.

'Quiet,' I shouted and the entire boat fell silent.

Llywelyn tried to move and the wave rocked the boat from side to side. 'I can move my tail but it's the rest of me that's stuck. If you could just give my tail a tug...'

'You're in a right pickle. What on earth can we do?' said Huw as Llywelyn splashed and wriggled in the water. 'We'd better hurry,' he continued. 'I can see your skin beginning to dry out, and that's not good.'

'Couldn't we pull him free?' said Rhodri and Rhys for the umpteenth time.

'Will you stop repeating yourselves!' I said. 'We need a proper plan.'

Huw looked at the rats and then at me and then at some rope in the bottom of the boat. 'I've got an idea: *we* could pull him free!'

Rhodri and Rhys folded their paws. 'What a great idea!' they said sarcastically.

Grabbing the rope, Huw tied a large loop at one end. 'If we can lasso this over his tail and tie the other end to the boat . . . I'll stick the motor in reverse and then some of us can push and some of us can pull.'

I passed the rope to the front of the boat and Sir Francis tied it on with a nautical knot. Without being asked, Rhodri and Rhys grabbed the rope in their teeth and dived into the water. Within seconds, they'd slipped the loop over Llywelyn's tail and jumped back in the boat.

Then Sir Francis and the All Quacks fluttered into the water and divided themselves between the front of the boat and Llywelyn's head. 'Get ready!' I shouted. The All Quacks all quacked, Cardigan crossed his hooves, the pigeon crossed his wings and Huw put the motor into reverse.

The engine throbbed, the ducks pushed and the water started to swirl but Llywelyn was still firmly wedged on the sandbank.

'Push harder,' shouted Huw as he increased the motor's speed but still Llywelyn didn't move.

Suddenly the rats jumped back into the sea and joined the ducks. They started to push and push and push and kick their little legs as hard as they could.

Slowly, very slowly, Llywelyn started to move. Bit by bit, he began to slide off the sandbank. 'That's it,' he boomed. 'That's it!'

With the motor at full speed and ducks and rats pushing, suddenly there was a giant splash and the boat shot backward. Llywelyn was free.

Huw stopped the motor and Rhodri and Rhys removed the rope. As they scrambled back on board, everyone clapped.

'That was brilliant,' I said to them. 'Well done, everybody, and well done especially to you two rats. You saved the day.'

Chapter Seven

We chugged our way back to the slipway with Llywelyn chatting as he swam alongside us. 'Many thanks,' he said. 'It was stupid of me to get stuck. That sandbank caught me out today.'

'Are you OK to swim with us?' I asked. 'We don't want you to get stuck again.'

'Don't worry,' he said. 'It's deep water nearly all the way to the RNLI boathouse. Are you here on holiday?'

'Yes. We are from the St Mary Dairy in Pont-y-cary,' said Rhys. 'Where are you from?'

'From Wales,' he said. 'Llywelyn Fawr is my name, Llywelyn the Great.'

'Really,' said Rhodri, turning to me. 'So whales are from Wales, Nelson!'

'Yes,' I said. 'But turkeys still don't come from Turkey.'

'No, they don't, my little friend,' said Llywelyn. 'But I am a real Welsh whale; I have lived off the coast for years.' He looked ahead of him. 'Normally I try to keep away from people, but look...' He pointed a huge flipper.

We all turned and looked at the crowd cheering the boat. As we docked, the cheering and clapping got louder. The mayor of Tenby was waiting for us, along with a coastguard, James Pond and hundreds of people.

'Well done,' said the mayor. 'We have been watching you. What a rescue!'

'We often watch the whales,' said the coastguard. 'We had just spotted that one was stuck but you got to him first. Congratulations!'

A huge spray of water shot up from Llywelyn and soaked everyone as he swam away. 'Thank you again,' he called behind him. '*Diolch yn fawr.*'

Rhodri and Rhys ran to wave goodbye. 'Will we see you again?'

'Maybe,' called Llywelyn. And, with that, he was gone.

'I hope he comes back,' sniffed Rhys.

'Do you think he would like to visit us at Pont-y-cary?' asked Rhodri.

'I expect he would,' I said. 'Not sure where he could stay though.'

'In the pond,' said Rhys excitedly.

'Might be a bit of a squeeze,' I smiled.

Ms Pugh the View had heard the news. In fact a TV crew was reporting the rescue as we arrived at the guest house and other radio and newspaper reporters were waiting outside. They all started talking at once.

Ms Pugh held up her hand for silence. 'Why doesn't everyone come in for a cup of tea and you can all take turns to interview the Tenby Heroes.'

'*The Tenby Heroes*. Great headline,' said a journalist, writing it down.

'It was Rhodri and Rhys – they really did the rescuing,' I said.

'Rats Rescue Welsh Whales,' said the journalist. 'I love it!'

'Everybody inside!' said Ms Pugh, folding her arms. 'Not another word.' And everyone trooped into Trem y Môr guest house.

It took a long time to tell the whole story. Rhodri and Rhys had their photo taken and were filmed for TV. I was interviewed, the ducks were interviewed, and even Flight Lieutenant Pigeon was interviewed. Sadly he was facing the wrong way when the broadcast appeared.

We all went to bed very late that night after a special dinner made by Ms Pugh. She called it a Sea View Pugh Stew...lovely.

Very early next day there was a knock at the guest-house door, followed by some voices outside my stable. When I looked out, there was the mayor, Huw and the coastguard.

'Good morning, Nelson,' said the mayor. 'We would like to thank you all for your help in the great whale rescue and so we have organised a special lunch at the RNLI station. Please say you will be our guests of honour.'

It only took a matter of moments to wake the rest of the gang and explain what was going on and, at midday, we all trotted, hopped or waddled our way to the lifeboat station. There, waiting for us, was the party to end all parties. The kind people of Tenby had thought of everything, from nosebags of fresh hay for Cardigan and me, to cucumber sandwiches for the lifeboat crew. We all sat down and ate and drank and chatted and laughed. But there was someone missing, and soon I saw Rhodri and Rhys hanging over the railings staring at the sea.

'It's Llywelyn's party really,' said Rhys. 'Do you think he will come and see us?'

'A whale is a wild animal,' I explained. 'He could be hundreds of miles away by now. He might have a family. Perhaps he's gone to look after them.'

They both looked a little sad.

'Whales are protected by law and people really shouldn't go near them. We were very lucky to meet one and help him but we will probably never see him close up again.'

They both sighed. 'OK. We understand.'

We sat down again and Rhodri was just helping himself to his seventh slice of pizza when... a huge spray of water showered onto our side of the table. Dripping wet, Rhodri and Rhys ran back to the railings. 'It's him!' they shouted. 'It's Llywelyn.'

It was indeed, but Llywelyn was not alone. Two mighty whales were looking up at the wet guests.

'Hello, my friends,' said Llywelyn, swimming in a circle. 'This is my wife, Bronwen, and somewhere, underwater, are Dai and Nerys, our little ones.'

Two baby fin whales suddenly splashed out of the sea and quickly back in again, sending a fountain of water into the air.

'Little ones!' muttered Cardigan. 'That's an understatement.'

The rats squealed with delight. 'We knew you'd come back.'

'Well, I just wanted to introduce the family. And we could smell the pizza from miles away.'

'Whales eat pizza?' we all said.

'Only if it has anchovies,' said Llywelyn. 'Pepperoni makes me burp and you don't want to be around when a whale burps!'

It was a wonderful afternoon. Llywelyn chatted to the rats and posed for photographs whilst the baby whales played in the sea, watched by their mother. But all too soon, the party came to an end and everybody had to go home. Rhodri and Rhys gave Llywelyn their address and they both promised to send Christmas cards. Although I did wonder how the postman was going to cope with Mr Ll. Whale, the Irish Sea!

Once the party was over, we all went back to the guest house to pack.

'Call me when you are ready to go,' said James Pond as he hopped off to have one last shower. He'd spend all day in there if he could.

It wasn't long before Ivor the Driver was tapping on the door.

Ms Pugh hugged us all. 'Life will be so quiet without you,' she said. 'You will come back, won't you?'

I couldn't resist it. 'Whale meet again,' I said.

Everybody groaned.

The whole of Tenby came out to see us off and the last thing we saw were some giant flippers waving from the sea as we drove away from the harbour.

The journey home was quiet. Nearly everybody fell asleep, all except me. I knew that I might have a slight problem waiting for me...Mike.

But, when we arrived, as luck would have it, Mike hadn't yet got back and there was no sign of Merv the Milk. Ivor the Driver was a little surprised to

see the speed with which everyone leapt out of the bus. Cases flew through the air as we hurriedly said our goodbyes and fled.

'Right,' I said. 'We don't want Mike finding out that we spent the weekend in Tenby or we'll be in terrible trouble. We must make sure he doesn't see anything in the press about our little rescue. Rhodri, check to see if the Sunday papers have been delivered and get rid of them. Rhys, find the radio in the kitchen and take the batteries out. Flight Lieutenant Pigeon, fly up to the roof and loosen the TV aerial . . . that should do it.'

Cardigan nodded his approval. 'Smart thinking; now let's get to bed and look as if we have been here all weekend. Oh, and leave the kitchen window open. Make it all look normal.'

With all the little jobs done, everyone settled down. The ducks rested in the reeds. Flight Lieutenant Pigeon roosted in the rafters. Rhodri and Rhys snuggled down in the straw and Cardigan was soon snoring.

It must have been quite late when Mike came home. I pretended to be asleep but watched out of one eye as he checked us all and then went into his kitchen. I could hear him trying the telly and tapping the radio and even tutting and muttering that the papers hadn't been delivered. Finally he went to bed.

It must have been about 11 o'clock when the phone rang in the

kitchen...and rang...and rang. Eventually I heard a sleepy Mike saying, 'Hello? Ms Pugh the View? Who? Tenby? In the shower? What? Hang on!'

Everybody was awake by the time the back door flew open and Mike pounded across the yard. I sat there blinking as he flicked on my stable light.

Mike did not look happy. 'Why have I just had a call from a Ms Pugh of the Sea View guest house in Tenby?' he stormed. 'She said that there is a frog in a bow tie in the shower and she can't get him out!'

OH YOGHURTS! I knew there was something I had forgotten...